With thanks to all at the Bafran Arab Stud, Spiez, Switzerland

Chestnut Grey copyright © Frances Lincoln 1993
Text and illustrations copyright © Helen Cooper 1993

First published in Great Britain in 1993 by
Frances Lincoln Limited, 4 Torriano Mews,
Torriano Avenue, London NW5 2RZ

First paperback edition 2000

British Library Cataloguing in Publication Data available on request

ISBN 0-7112-1552-9 paperback

Printed in Hong Kong

1 3 5 7 9 8 6 4 2

Helen Cooper was born in London and brought up in Cumbria.
After studying for a Diploma at the Royal College of Music,
she decided to develop her self-taught skills as an illustrator. Her first book,
Kit and the Magic Kite (Hamish Hamilton) was published in 1986.
Now a full-time author and illustrator of children's books, her titles include
Ella and the Rabbit (Frances Lincoln), *The Bear Under the Stairs*
(Doubleday), which was shortlisted for the 1994 Kate Greenaway Medal
and won the Young Judge's Award for the Smarties Book Prize in 1993,
The Baby Who Wouldn't Go to Bed (Doubleday), which won
the 1996 Kate Greenaway Medal and *Pumpkin Soup* (Doubleday),
which won the Kate Greenaway Medal 1998 and was
shortlisted for the Kurt Maschler Award.
Helen lives in North London with her husband and daughter.

Chestnut Grey

A folk tale from Russia

Helen Cooper

FRANCES LINCOLN

A man once bought himself a farm and moved in with his three sons, well pleased with his beautiful new barley field. But he wasn't pleased very long. On Midsummer's Eve something came, and gobbled, and trampled the barley field flat.

Well, this happened once, and it happened twice, and the poor farmer didn't know what to do.

"*I'll* catch the thief," said the eldest son. "I'll watch the field all night from the barn." And the second son agreed to go too.

Ivan the youngest son thought his own thoughts and said nothing, for no one ever listened to him.

It was warm and drowsy in the barn when the two eldest sons crept in that night. They had promised not even to close their eyes, but the straw was so soft that soon they slept.

The next day the field looked a terrible mess.

"But we didn't sleep a wink!" they lied.

"Ivan shall watch the field tonight," said the poor farmer. "But he's so useless, he's bound to do even worse than you!"

Ivan said nothing, just thought his own thoughts. But that night he didn't go into the barn. He held a rope in one hand, a bread bun in the other, and sat in the gloom wide-eyed and munching.

Just as the clock struck midnight, a magical horse thundered into the field. So swiftly he galloped, sparks flew from his hooves. So swiftly, the sky seemed to reel and shake.

The horse began to eat,
and he trampled even more than he ate.
But Ivan stole up, threw a rope round his neck,
and quick as a wink was astride his back.
How that horse did buck and kick,
how he reared and galloped,
screamed and pranced!
But Ivan laughed and held on tight,
and though they battled half the night,
the horse couldn't throw him off.

At last the horse gave up the fight. "If only you'll let me go,"
he pleaded, "I'll come to your aid whenever you need me."

"First," insisted Ivan sternly, "give me your solemn word that you'll
never spoil our barley again."

The horse bowed his head and promised. "Remember this,"
he said. "If ever you need me, just clap your hands three times and say
    Chestnut Grey, hear and obey!
and I'll be there before you can blink."

When Ivan told of all he had done, his family fell about laughing.

"A talking horse?" they mocked. "What nonsense!"

Nonsense or not, the barley field was never trampled again, but Ivan got no thanks for that.

Far away in the city, strange news was astir. Princess Elena the Fair had declared she would only marry the horseman who could leap up to her high window and take the ring from her finger.

Nothing would change her mind. The king was in despair. So he sent out his heralds to announce a day when all the horsemen in the land might try to win the princess's hand.

The two older brothers thought themselves very fine horsemen, and they boasted their fortunes were made.

Ivan sat quietly and said nothing. Secretly he didn't think much of their bragging, and he was relieved when they left.

He strolled out to a quiet glade, clapped his hands three times and called,
Chestnut Grey, hear and obey!
Before his voice had died away, into the glade galloped Chestnut Grey. He circled once and came to a halt before Ivan.

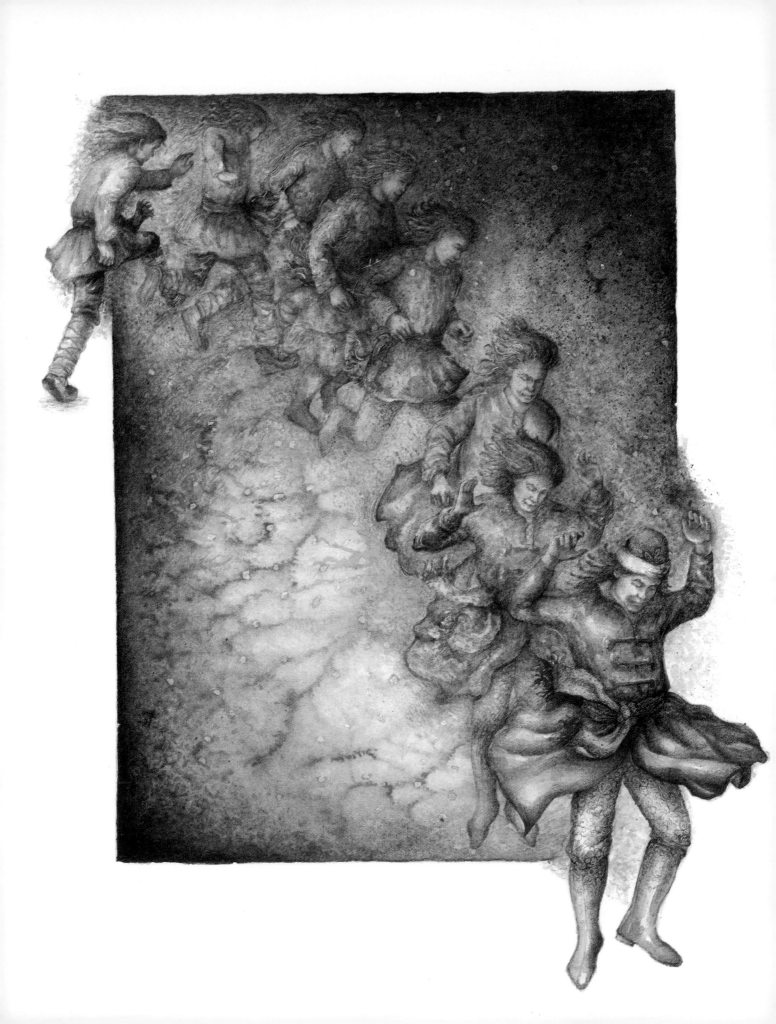

"I thought you'd call," snorted Chestnut Grey, "and now it's time to be on our way. For I can jump as high as a hayrick, as high as a house, as high as a forest." And he lashed the air with his swirling tail.

"But I can't meet the princess like this," complained Ivan, looking down at his torn clothes.

"No, you can't go in those," agreed Chestnut Grey, "but climb into my left ear and out through my right, and then we'll see."

"Climb into your ear?" gasped Ivan. "How can I?"

"Just try," said Chestnut Grey.

So Ivan tried. To his surprise, it was the easiest thing in the world, and he came out dressed like a prince.

"Now we're ready!" cried Chestnut Grey, and they galloped away to the city.

In the centre of the city was a busy square, in the square was a tower, and right at the tip-top window of that tower sat Princess Elena the Fair. She looked beautiful enough to make your heart stop.

All the young men gathered there. They galloped and leaped, and leaped and galloped, until their fine horses were all in a lather — but not one could get near the princess.

Then Chestnut Grey raced into the square. He snorted and leaped up into the sky, higher than any of the other horses, high enough even to clear a house, but not high enough to reach the princess's window.

"Quick! Let's be off," whispered Ivan, and away they sped before anyone could stop them.

"That tower is a ridiculous height!" grumbled Ivan's brothers when they came home that night. "Only one man got anywhere near, and after one leap even he disappeared."

"Maybe I should come tomorrow," said Ivan from his fireside chair.

"You wouldn't stand a chance," they scoffed. "And what princess would look at you?"

Ivan said nothing, just thought his own thoughts. But next day he summoned Chestnut Grey, climbed into the horse's left ear and out through the right, and came out even more splendidly dressed than the first time.

There was silence as they raced into the square. Chestnut Grey snorted, and leaped up into the sky. Higher than any of the other horses, high enough even to clear a forest, but still not quite high enough to reach the princess's window.

On the last day of the contest, Ivan summoned Chestnut Grey one more time. "Today you must jump as you've never jumped before!" he pleaded.

The horse nodded his great head, and lashed the air with his wild tail. Then they galloped into the city, and on into the square.

Chestnut Grey snorted, and leaped to the sky. Higher than any other horse, higher than ever he'd leaped before, high enough for Ivan to kiss the princess, and take the ring from her finger.

The crowd cheered and whistled and waved — they all wanted to greet the champion. But Ivan got away. They could not find him anywhere.

Three whole days went by, and the princess's future bridegroom was nowhere to be found. Ivan was hiding himself away with a rag wrapped around the ring on his finger. He tried not to think of the princess, for surely no princess would want to marry an ordinary farmer's son.

But once more the king sent his heralds out, to every part of the land. He commanded all his subjects to attend a grand banquet. No one dared disobey, and even Ivan had to be there.

All the guests were seated at oak tables laden with food. But Ivan withdrew to a shadowy corner, well away from the feasting.

Elena the Fair moved among the guests. She searched every table, she searched every face without success. Then, in the darkest corner of all, she found Ivan.

"Take that rag off your hand," she said with a smile.

Ivan unwound the rag, and there, to everyone's surprise, sparkled the princess's ring. The princess didn't mind his old torn clothes – she just led him up to the king. And the king welcomed Ivan into his family.

For the last time, Ivan summoned Chestnut Grey, and his old rags melted away and were transformed into wedding clothes.

Then Chestnut Grey proudly carried Ivan and his beautiful bride to the church.

MORE PICTURE BOOKS IN PAPERBACK
FROM FRANCES LINCOLN

ELLA AND THE RABBIT
Helen Cooper

Early one morning, Ella decides to visit her daddy's champion rabbit by herself.
Surely it wouldn't be naughty just to open the cage door a tiny crack. This charming
cautionary tale for under-fives is brought to life with realistic and stylish illustrations.
Nominated for the 1991 Kate Greenaway Medal.

Suitable for National Curriculum English – Reading, Key Stage 1
Scottish Guidelines English Language – Reading, Level A

ISBN 0-7112-0635-X £4.99

THE EMPEROR AND THE NIGHTINGALE
Meilo So

This striking new version of the Hans Christian Anderson tale, beautifully retold,
combines dazzling artwork with a read-aloud text. Meilo So's bold water-colours
convincingly evoke the elaborate atmosphere of the Chinese Emperor's court.

Suitable for National Curriculum English – Reading, Key Stage 1
Scottish Guidelines English Language – Reading, Level B

ISBN 0-7112-1416-6 £4.99

THE MONKEY AND THE PANDA
Antonia Barber
Illustrated by Meilo So

Lean, lively Monkey plays naughty tricks and makes the village children laugh.
But in their quieter moments the children prefer the company of fat,
friendly Panda. This original story cleverly combines allegory with fun
and will enchant animal lovers everywhere.

Suitable for National Curriculum English – Reading, Key Stages 1 and 2
Scottish Guidelines English Language – Reading, Level C

ISBN 0-7112-1085-3 £4.99

Frances Lincoln titles are available from all good bookshops.

Prices are correct at the time of publication, but may be subject to change.